**Stephanie Blake**'s passion for writing and illustrating began in childhood when she created books for her brothers and sisters as birthday presents. As a child, she also fell in love with the books of Dr. Seuss, Ludwig Bemelmans, and William Steig. After moving to France, she discovered other writers and artists whose works continued to inspire her stories and drawings. Stephanie is the author and illustrator of dozens of books, including *Poop-di-doop!* and *Super Bunny!* She lives in Paris, France.

First published in the United States and Canada in 2015 by NorthSouth Books, Inc.,
an imprint of Nord-Süd Verlag AG, CH-8005 Zürich, Switzerland.

Distributed in the United States by NorthSouth Books, Inc., New York 10016.
Library of Congress Cataloging-in-Publication Data is available.

ISBN: 978-0-7358-4255-7
Printed in China by Leo Paper Products Ltd., Heshan, Guangdong, September 2015.
1  3  5  7  9  •  10  8  6  4  2

www.northsouth.com

## Stephanie Blake

# New Baby!

North
South

# Simon
## just built
## a
## very,
## very,
## very
# BIG
## rocket.

# CRASH!

It collapsed
in
a
heap.

# "SHHHH!"
said Simon's mother.
"You need to play
more quietly.
We have a
tiny
new baby
in the house."

**Simon peeked into the baby's room and said, "Go home, New Baby!"**

# Suddenly, Simon started to think:

"When is it going back to the hospital?" Simon asked. "Simon! This is your baby brother. You know he's here to stay!"

"Forever!?!"
"Yes, forever,
my dear little one."

"Good night, my little bunny,"
said his mother.
"Good night, my little bunny,"
said his father.
"Good night," said Simon.
"Did you kiss me?" asked Simon.
"Of course I did, my dear,"
said his mother.
"I want another kiss,"
begged Simon.
So his mother gave him
another kiss,
and his father gave him
another kiss.
Simon closed his eyes,
but he couldn't fall asleep.
He lay in bed awake
for hours.

Then he started thinking
about the wolf.

# The
# BIG
# bad
# wolf.

He thought about big wolves
and little wolves,
wolf fathers
and wolf mothers,
wolf sisters
and wolf brothers,
and wolf babies!
Suddenly,
Simon was absolutely certain
he was surrounded
by thousands of wolves.

A thousand million
BIG
BAD
WOLVES
who would
eat him up.

Simon
jumped out of bed
and ran to his
parents' bedroom.
They were sound asleep.
He stood there quietly
without making a sound.
"Go back to bed,
my little bunny,"
said his father.
"I can't! There are wolves
in my room.
Can't I sleep with you?"
asked Simon.
"GO TO BED, SIMON!"
So Simon went back
to his room.

**In the hallway,
Simon heard
funny little sounds:
GOOGOOS
and
GAGAS
and
BABYBOOS
and
BLATHERS.**

# "New Baby!"
### said Simon.

# "GOOGOOGAGABABY-BOOBLATHER!"
## answered his baby brother.

"You can't stay here!
The house is
full of
BIG
BAD
WOLVES.
I'm going to
protect you,
my
teeny-weeny
new baby."

**And that's exactly what he did.**